my many emotions

Happiness

Cherry Lake Press

Published in the United States of America by Cherry Lake Publishing Group
Ann Arbor, Michigan
www.cherrylakepublishing.com

Reading Adviser: Beth Walker Gambro, MS, Ed., Reading Consultant, Yorkville, IL
Content Adviser: Emily Fragapane, M.Ed., Ed.S., Nationally Certified School Psychologist, RYT200
Book Designer: Jennifer Wahi
Illustrator: Jeff Bane

Photo Credits: © Inside Creative House/Shutterstock.com, 5; © narikan/Shutterstock.com, 7; © Photographee.eu/Shutterstock.com, 9; © varuna/Shutterstock.com, 11; © Africa Studio/Shutterstock.com, 13; © Svitlana Bezuhlova/Shutterstock.com, 15; © prostock-studio/Shutterstock.com, 17; © AnaLysiSStudiO/Shutterstock.com, 19; © Rido/Shutterstock.com, 21; © Monkey Business Images/Shutterstock.com, 23; Cover, 2-3, 6, 12, 22, 24, Jeff Bane

Cherry Lake Press is an imprint of Cherry Lake Publishing Group.

Library of Congress Cataloging-in-Publication Data

Names: Devera, Czeena, author. | Bane, Jeff, 1957- illustrator.
Title: Happiness / by Czeena Devera ; illustrated by Jeff Bane.
Description: Ann Arbor, Michigan : Cherry Lake Publishing, [2021] | Series: My many emotions | Includes index. | Audience: Grades K-1
Identifiers: LCCN 2021004896 (print) | LCCN 2021004897 (ebook) | ISBN 9781534186927 (hardcover) | ISBN 9781534188327 (paperback) | ISBN 9781534189720 (pdf) | ISBN 9781534191129 (ebook)
Subjects: LCSH: Happiness--Juvenile literature. | Emotional intelligence--Juvenile literature. | Social learning--Juvenile literature.
Classification: LCC BF575.H27 D48 2021 (print) | LCC BF575.H27 (ebook) | DDC 152.4/2--dc23
LC record available at https://lccn.loc.gov/2021004896
LC ebook record available at https://lccn.loc.gov/2021004897

Printed in the United States of America
Corporate Graphics

table of contents

Happiness 4

Glossary 24

Index 24

About the author: Czeena Devera grew up in the red-hot heat of Arizona surrounded by books. Her childhood bedroom had built-in bookshelves that were always full. She now lives in Michigan with an even bigger library of books.

About the illustrator: Jeff Bane and his two business partners own a studio along the American River in Folsom, California, home of the 1849 Gold Rush. When Jeff's not sketching or illustrating for clients, he's either swimming or kayaking in the river to relax.

You know the feeling when your cheeks hurt from smiling? It's a good kind of hurt. That's **Happiness**.

How would you describe Happiness?

Happiness can be slow and **steady**. Or it can come in **bursts**, like a laugh.

Happiness can come when you're waiting for your birthday. It's an exciting time.

You might feel Happiness when the sun shines. You might feel this **especially** after a few rainy days!

How does Happiness feel to you?

Your body might feel like it's buzzing with **energy**. Maybe you feel butterflies in your stomach.

Happiness is normal. It's also normal not to feel happy. There are things you can do to help.

Write down a few things you are thankful for. **Gratitude** can make us feel happy!

Helping people can lead to Happiness. You can pick up a classmate's pencil if they drop it. Or let someone go in front of you in line.

Happiness is meant to be shared. Smile at a stranger. Or share good news with a friend.

How do you show Happiness?

When you feel Happiness, enjoy it! Remember to share it with others.

glossary & index

glossary

bursts (BURSTS) short, fast starts of something, such as an emotion

energy (EN-ur-jee) the strength to do active things

especially (ess-PESH-uh-lee) more than usual, in particular

gratitude (GRAT-uh-tood) a state of being thankful

happiness (HAH-pee-nuhss) a state of well-being

steady (STED-ee) a state of little to no change

index

body, 12
good, 4, 20
happy, 14, 16
laugh, 6
share, 20, 22
smile, 4, 20